What's the Magic Word?

By Kelly DiPucchio

Illustrated by Marsha Winborn

HarperCollinsPublishers

In a tree, in a nest,
on a gusty spring morn,
a speckled egg cracked,
and a small bird was born.

A wind spun round, making blossoms fly,

and WHOOSHED Little Bird up into the sky!

He swirled through the air in a blustery squall . . .

and he landed KERPLUNK by a hay-filled . . .

. . . STALL.

"Hello? Hello? Can I come in?"
"What's the magic word, Little Bird?"

"Peep-peep?"

"No, no. Haven't you heard?

Moo-moo

is the magic word, silly Little Bird!"

Then a wind spun round, making milk pails fly,

and WHOOSHED Little Bird back into the sky!

He flew by the farmer, out for a drive . . .

I ♥ Moocows

and he landed KERPLUNK

by a big, buzzing . . .

. . . HIVE.

"Hello? Hello? Can I come in?"

"What's the magic word, Little Bird?"

"Moo-moo?"

"No, no. Haven't you heard?

Buzz-buzz

is the magic word, silly Little Bird!"

Then a wind spun round, making honeysuckle fly,

and WHOOSHED Little Bird back into the sky!

He whirled through a windmill, round and round . . .

and he landed KERPLUNK by the house of a . . .

. . . HOUND.

"Hello? Hello? Can I come in?"

"What's the magic word, Little Bird?"

"Buzz-buzz?"

"No, no. Haven't you heard?

BOW-WOW

is the magic word, silly Little Bird!"

Then a wind spun round, making dandelions fly,

and WHOOSHED Little Bird back into the sky!

He swooped through the underwear swaying on the line . . .

and he landed KERPLUNK by a tall, hollow . . .

. . . PINE.

"Hello? Hello? Can I come in?"

"What's the magic word, Little Bird?"

"Bow-wow?"

"No, no. Haven't you heard?

Hoo-hoo

is the magic word, silly Little Bird!"

Then a wind spun round, making long johns fly,

and WHOOSHED Little Bird back into the sky!

He bounced off Mrs. Brown's blueberry pie . . .

and he landed KERPLUNK by a sloppy mud . . .

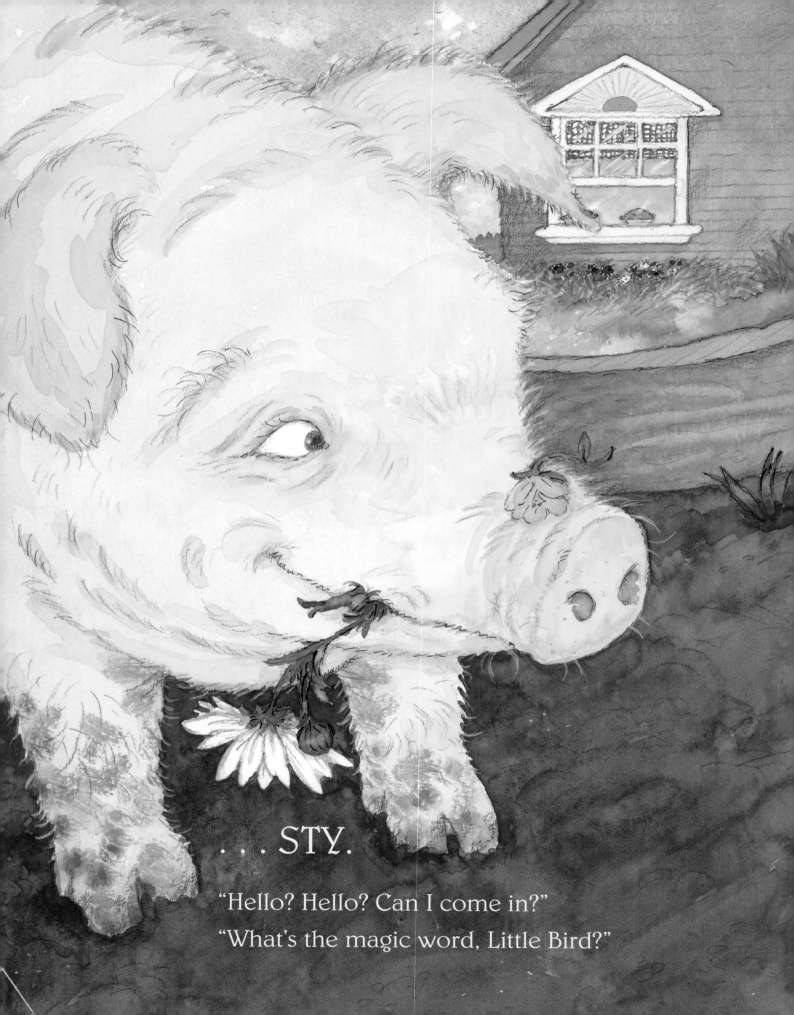

. . . STY.

"Hello? Hello? Can I come in?"
"What's the magic word, Little Bird?"

"Hoo-hoo?"

"No, no. Haven't you heard?
Oink-oink
is the magic word, silly Little Bird!"

Then a wind spun round, making fruit pies fly,

and WHOOSHED Little Bird back into the sky!

The gusty winds changed from east to west . . .

and Little Bird landed KERPLUNK by a cozy twig . . .

. . . NEST.

"Hello, hello . . . "

"Little Bird, Little Bird!
Where have you been?"

"Mama Bird, Mama Bird! Can I come in?"

"Of course, Little Bird. What's the magic word?"

"Oink-oink?
Hoo-hoo?
Bow-wow?
Buzz...moo?"

"Come in, Little Bird. Get out of that breeze!
And haven't you heard?
The magic word is . . .

"Please!"

To my mom and dad, for giving me wings to fly
—K.D.

What's the Magic Word?
Text copyright © 2005 by Kelly DiPucchio
Illustrations copyright © 2005 by Marsha Winborn
Manufactured in China by South China Printing Company Ltd.
All rights reserved.
www.harperchildrens.com

Library of Congress Cataloging-in-Publication Data
DiPucchio, Kelly S.
 What's the magic word? / by Kelly DiPucchio ; illustrated by Marsha Winborn.— 1st
ed.
  p. cm.
 Summary: As a newly hatched bird is blown around the farmyard by a strong wind,
he keeps learning passwords that will allow him to enter different animal's homes, but
is blown away again before he has the chance to go in.
 ISBN 0-06-000578-5 — ISBN 0-06-000579-3 (lib. bdg.)
 [1. Birds—Fiction. 2. Domestic animals—Fiction. 3. Animals—Fiction. 4. Winds—
Fiction. 5. Stories in rhyme.] I. Title: What is the magic word? II. Winborn, Marsha, ill.
III. Title.
PZ8.3.D5998Wha 2005   2003026549
[E]—dc22

Typography by Elynn Cohen   1 2 3 4 5 6 7 8 9 10 ❖ First Edition